Original
Sylvanian families™

FOREST EVERGREEN'S
BIRTHDAY SURPRISE
Simon Harwood

FANTAIL

FOREST EVERGREEN was a very lucky man. He had a lovely wife, Honeysuckle. He also had four beautiful children: Ashley, Preston, Summer and Logan. They all respected him and loved their father very much.

"It'll soon be Daddy's birthday," said Ashley. "What shall we get him."

THE children emptied out all their money boxes. Between them, they had less than a pound.

"Oh, no!" they wailed. "What are we going to do?" The children sat around wondering what they could buy their father with such a small amount of money.

"I know," said Ashley. "You know how Dad loves to put his feet up in the evening and how Mum gets mad at him for putting them on her best chairs." "Yes," they all said. "Well, how about it if we make him a little footstool, so he wouldn't get into any more trouble?"

"BRILLIANT," said Logan. "I've got some wood in the shed and I'm sure Grandfather Ernest will help us with nails and tools." So Logan ran off to find his Grandfather. Grandfather Ernest is an inventor and is always pottering in his workshop so Logan knew where to find him. Grandfather Ernest was happy to help. Logan ran back to tell his brother and sisters the good news.

"WE'LL need a cushion for the top of the stool," said Preston. "I'll ask Grandmother Primrose if she'll help us. She knows just what to do with needle and cotton, and I'm sure she's got some material we could use."

"What a good idea," they all agreed.

"BUT where can we make it, so Daddy won't find out?" asked Summer.

"Let's make it in my bedroom and we'll put a No Entry sign on the door," said Logan. "Whatever happens, Dad must not find out or it will ruin the surprise completely." Off they all scurried to get started.

LATER that evening as Forest Evergreen sat by the fire, he said to his wife, "You know my dear, it's a funny thing. I went to say goodnight to Logan and his door had a No Entry sign on it. He would not let me in."

"Oh," smiled Honeysuckle, "children go through these funny phases. Maybe he thinks he's too old for a goodnight kiss, dear. And please can you take your feet off my best armchair."

AS Forest Evergreen's birthday approached, Logan's bedroom became a hive of activity. Grandfather Ernest went in with bits of wood, a saw and some tools. What a noise they made, particularly when Ernest hit his thumb with a hammer instead of the nail.

GRANDMOTHER PRIMROSE bustled in and out of the bedroom carrying her basket with bits of material and padding. She spent many hours in there with Ashley and Summer busily sewing away. Ashley and Summer loved spending time with Primrose because she was so good at forecasting the weather. If her ears tingle, it will be sunny, if her toes itch, it will be rainy. Luckily on the day before Forest's birthday, her ears were tingling.

BUT all this time, Forest had been forbidden entry into Logan's bedroom. Whenever Forest went to say goodnight, his way was barred. He began to wonder what he had done wrong.

"I must have been too hard on the boy. I shouldn't have stopped his pocket money that time he broke a window playing football. After all, boy bears will be boy bears. I dare say I must have broken a few windows in my time," Forest thought to himself.

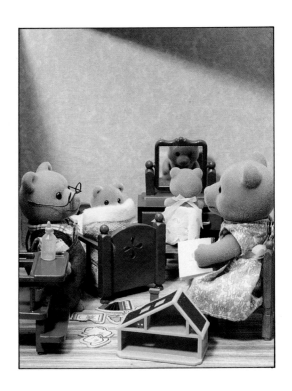

LATER that evening while Honey-suckle was reading to the babies, Dusty and Poppy, their favourite story, and playing a game of peek-a-boo, Ernest came in and said to Honeysuckle, "Oh, the sooner Forest finds out what's going on the better. He looks a really worried man."

FINALLY the day of Forest's birthday dawned. But Forest was feeling very sad. He was certain that he had been far too strict as a father. Even Honeysuckle's lovely present of a yellow and blue polka dot bow-tie didn't cheer him up.

"My children will hate me, especially Logan," he murmured to himself. "How can I possibly enjoy my birthday?"

BUT just then Logan popped his head around the sitting room door.

"Dad, I think it's time I explained why I haven't let you into my room for so long," he said.

"It's alright, son, I understand," said Forest. "I haven't been as good a father as I thought."

"Nonsense," said Logan. "You're the best father in the world. That's why we wanted to make this a really special surprise for your birthday."

THEN the others piled into the room carrying Forest's footstool. It was a real work of craftsmanship. The legs were made of oak and the top was covered by a beautifully embroidered cushion. Ashley put her father's feet on it.

"Now you can put your feet up whenever you want," they all cried. "Do you like it?"

"IT'S the nicest, most wonderful birthday present I've ever had in my whole life," laughed Forest, sneakily wiping away a happy tear.

"We love you, Dad," they all said. "Happy birthday."

FANTAIL PUBLISHING, AN IMPRINT OF PUFFIN ENTERPRISES

Published by the Penguin Group
27 Wrights Lane, London W8 5TZ, England
Viking Penguin Inc., 40 West 23rd Street, New York, NY 10010, USA
Penguin Books Australia Ltd, Ringwood, Victoria, Australia
Penguin Books Canada Ltd, 2801 John Street, Markham, Ontario,
Canada L3R 1B4
Penguin Books (NZ) Ltd, 182-190 Wairau Road, Auckland 10, New Zealand
Penguin Books Ltd, Registered Offices: Harmondsworth,
Middlesex, England

First published by Fantail Publishing, 1988

Copyright © 1988 Epoch Co LTD
All rights reserved

014 0900012

Made and printed in Great Britain by

William Clowes Limited
Beccles and London